W9-CJL-416

# WILEY & GRAMPA'S CREATURE FEATURES

# BIGFOOT BACKPACKING BONANZA

WRITTEN AND ILLUSTRATED BY

## KIRK SCROGGS

THE CALL OF THE WILD!

THE SMELL OF DE-FEET!

 LITTLE, BROWN AND COMPANY

New York ⚭ Boston

*This book is for Morgan*

———

Special thanks to:
Ashley & Carolyn Grayson, Suppasak Viboonlarp, Mark
Mayes, Jim Jeong, Joe Kocian, Hiland Hall, Steve Deline, Inge, Alejandra, Beth &
Laura at B&N, Dav Pilkey, Jackie Greed, and the mezz crew—Woo Woo!

Andrea, Jill, Sangeeta, Saho, Alison, Elizabeth, Tina,
and the Little, Brown crew—hooray!

And a super deep-dish thanks with extra cheese to Diane and Corey
Scroggs and Harold and Betty Aulds.

Little, Brown and Company

Hachette Book Group USA
237 Park Avenue, New York, NY 10169
Visit our Web site at www.lb-kids.com

First Edition: May 2007

ISBN-13:978-0-316-05948-0 (hc) / ISBN-10: 0-316-05948-X (hc)
ISBN-13: 978-0-316-05949-7 (pb) / ISBN-10: 0-316-05949-8 (pb)

10 9 8 7 6 5 4 3 2 1

CW

Printed in the United States of America

Series design by Saho Fujii

The illustrations for this book were done in Staedtler ink on Canson Marker paper,
then digitized with Adobe Photoshop for color and shade.
The text was set in Humana Sans Light and the display type was handlettered.

# CHAPTERS

# CHAPTER 1

# This Spud's for You

We interrupt this broadcast for an emergency news flash. Criminal mastermind Hans Lotion and his grandson, Jurgen, have escaped from their maximum security facility. Hans is a master of explosives and funny accents and is extremely dangerous. If you spot these two, contact the police, alert the media, or just wave your hands in the air and scream like a stuck pig!

*We now return to*
***Terminator 7:***
***Cyborgs In Love...***

No, wait! That's not a killer cyborg.

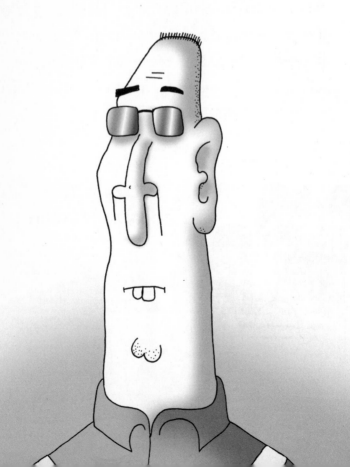

That's Mr. Gorden Maximus, owner of the biggest shoe store in town and Scoutleader of the Spudscouts of America.

"Only a few lucky elite can become a Spudscout!" barked Spudmaster Maximus. "It takes nerves of steel, a perfect physique, like mine, and a real smart brain."

"Now, what makes you two puny maggots think you've got what it takes to be Spudscouts?"

Those two puny maggots he was referring to were me, Wiley, and my best friend, Jubal. This was our fifth time trying out for Spudscouts, and it promised to be as humiliating as ever.

We were put through a serious of rigorous tests. First, we were forced to do pull-ups over a batch of dangerous insects.

Then came the exhausting swimming competition,

followed by a dangerous crawl through barbed-wire and muck, under scorching flames...

and topped off with an unbearable jalapeño-eating contest.

# CHAPTER 2

# The Long Walk of Shame

"I'm glad—I mean, sad—to say that for the fifth time, you two have failed to meet our standards," said Maximus. "But don't let this get you down. You can now proudly return to your daffodil garden on Wimp Island."

The creepy Spudscouts chuckled as we walked away.

"That does it," said Jubal. "Remind me not to invite these guys to my next birthday party."

Grampa tried to cheer us up later that night. "Hey boys!" said Grampa. "You're just in time for *N.Y.P.D.– Sasquatch Division*."

"No thanks," I said. "The thrill of watching a Sasquatch breaking bones is gone."

Gramma tried to cheer us up, too. "Boys, I made you a triple-decker chocolate brownie super sundae with a real working fountain of hot fudge."

"Sorry, Gramma," I said. "Not even a river of hot fudge could overcome the humiliation we're feeling right now."

"Uh, I'd be willing to give it a try," said Jubal.

Since we didn't make Spudscouts,
we settled for a crummy
overnight campout in my tree house.

"Don't worry, boys," said Grampa, from below.
"Winning isn't everything. The embarrassment
and feelings of utter worthlessness will go
away. It might take weeks, months, even years,
but they'll go away. Now have a good night."

"Well, Jubal," I said, "at least you were there to fail more miserably than I did. I can always count on you."

"Hey, anytime, buddy," said Jubal.

Soon, we drifted off to sleep.

# CHAPTER 3

# Packed with Excitement

We were awakened bright and early by a loud whistle and an even louder Grampa: "Rise and shine, sleepyheads! Up and at 'em! You've got gear to pack!"

"What kind of gear?" I asked.

"Camping gear, my friend. We don't need no stinkin' Spudscouts to rough it in the wilderness. I'll drag you through the woods myself."

So we packed up all the necessities and Merle, the cat, and took off on a grand adventure.

"Hold on to your drawers, gang," said Grampa. "We're on our way to the most rugged and dangerous spot in all of Texas."

# CHAPTER 4

# Rock Bottom

Gingham County State Park, home of the notorious Bigfoot and Texas' most famous rock formation...the Devil's Rump.

"The path up the **Devil's Rump** is extremely dangerous!" said Grampa. "Beware of large cracks, gusty winds, and dangerous mud slides!"

First, we had to set up camp. Grampa showed
me how to start a fire with two stones.

Then we put up our tents.

Merle caught dinner in a nearby stream.

And Gramma made a working microwave out of twigs and tree bark.

That night, over a roaring campfire, I
entertained everyone with horrifying stories of
lunatic summer camp counselors with hockey
masks and hooks for hands. But it was Gramma
who told the scariest story of all: "Tomorrow
night I'm going to cook you my world-famous
turnip and cottage cheese casserole."

"Like I said, boys," said Grampa, "we're really
roughing it out here."

# CHAPTER 5

# Grampa's Survival Guide

The next day, we set off on our hiking adventure.

"Before we enter the woods," said Grampa, "remember the four **R**'s of the wild: **R**attlesnakes, **R**ats, and **R**abid **R**accoons. The woods are full of 'em. Now let's go have a good time."

It was a morning full of adventure. We crossed
raging rivers, scaled steep cliffs...

slid down slippery slopes, hacked through thick vegetation, even did a little disco dancing. Everything was going great.

That is, until we fell face-first into a huge, weirdly shaped hole. But wait! That wasn't a hole—it was a gigantic footprint.

"This must be the footprint of the notorious Bigfoot!" said Grampa.

"How can you be sure?" I asked.

"Just look at this giant toenail clipping and that huge bottle of sparkly toenail polish."

# CHAPTER 6

# Grampa's Flashback Crunch

"This giant, crusty toenail clipping reminds me of the time I met Bigfoot," said Grampa.

"I was fresh out of the third grade, devastatingly handsome and looking for excitement. Boys my age across the country were joining the Spudscouts, so I did, too.

"One weekend we were challenged by our rivals, the Beansprouts, a mean and ugly bunch of brutes. Our challenge was simple. The first team to reach the top of the Devil's Rump and plant their flag would win the Silver Spud medal.

"Turned out the challenge was tougher than we thought. We waded through snake-infested rivers.

"We dodged enemy smoke bombs and water balloons as we crawled through the mud.

"We swam through murky swamp water.

"At night it would rain for hours and I would sit in my tent and write home to my folks or type in my blog.

"Then we reached the summit. While my men covered me with slingshot fire, I stormed the Devil's Rump with my flag in hand.

"But before I could reach the top, a huge bear jumped out to attack me!"

"We don't have bears in Texas," I interrupted.

"I know," said Grampa. "This was an escaped bear from the traveling Bavarian Circus—the most vicious kind of bear in the world, other than pandas, of course.

"Luckily, before the bear could snack on me, an even bigger creature jumped out of the woods! He was enormous and hairier than your Uncle Willie's lower back!

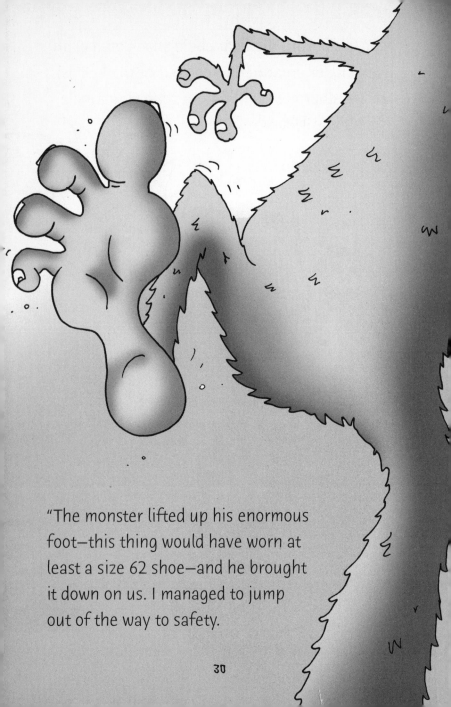

"The monster lifted up his enormous foot—this thing would have worn at least a size 62 shoe—and he brought it down on us. I managed to jump out of the way to safety.

30

"Then I ran, shrieking, all the way home. I lost my chance to win that Silver Spud Medal."

"What happened to the bear?" I asked.

"Well, I don't want to get too gross," said Grampa, "but when Bigfoot lifted his foot, that bear looked like raspberry jelly mixed with tapioca pudding. . . with little clumps of hair and crunchy bony bits—"

"Okay!" said Gramma. "I think we get the point."

# CHAPTER 7

# Let's Get Hairy

"Look at these enormous prints where Bigfoot sat on this rock!" said Jubal. "He must have an enormous—"

**But** Jubal's theory was cut short when Bigfoot himself jumped out of the forest! He was huge and hairy and had a shaggy skater-dude haircut.

"Don't worry!" yelled Grampa. "I'll lead you to safety. Just jump off this cliff into that raging river and everything will be okay!"

Luckily, Gramma served as a flotation device, so we all grabbed onto her and rode the rapids, leaving Bigfoot far behind.

"Look!" yelled Grampa. "This river rides right up the Devil's Rump!"

We lost all of our gear in the raging rapids and, to make things worse, we were headed straight for a huge waterfall. Certain doom and a whole lotta water awaited us.

"Well, this is it, gang!" said Grampa. "At least we were spared the turnip and cottage cheese casserole."

But, lucky for us, Spudmaster Maximus and his spooky Spudscouts were waiting at the bottom of the falls with a giant net.

"It's a good thing we've been monitoring your progress!" screamed Maximus. "Only experienced woodsmen or complete numbskulls should be in this area!"

# CHAPTER 8
# Club Dread

Maximus took us to his camp. "Welcome to Camp Hack 'n' Slash," said Maximus. "We just built it last night. We still have to put in plumbing and high-speed Internet."

The Spudscouts treated Gramma with extra care.

"I feel like the Queen of Sheba!" said Gramma.

"I don't trust these creeps," I whispered to Jubal.

"Me neither," said Jubal. "Just yesterday, that guy was shooting a flamethrower at us."

That night, the Spudscouts treated us to dinner.

"Tonight's menu is very special," said Maximus. "Tangy squirrel kabobs, roasted until they are slightly pink, with a side of chilled grub worms in a creamy mint sauce."

"Hey, as long as there's no mayonnaise on it," I said. I was pretty hungry.

We got our own luxury quarters for the night, while Gramma got a different cabin, but something just seemed fishy.

"Grampa, I don't trust Spudmaster Maximus."

"I don't know," said Grampa. "He seems nice . . . in an Attila the Hun kinda way."

Suddenly we heard a loud scream from outside.
It was Gramma! I tried to leave the room, but the
door and all of the windows were barred shut.

"They've locked us in!" I yelled. "And they've
taken Gramma!"

"Rats!" said Grampa. "I was just starting to get
comfortable."

# CHAPTER 9

# It's All Gone Kong

Gramma was tied to two posts over a cliff.

"Sorry, guys," said Spudmaster Maximus. "I need to borrow your beloved Gramma. I'm going to use her as bait to lure in the notorious Bigfoot. What hairy beast can resist a damsel in distress?"

"Then we'll shoot Bigfoot with this giant
tranquilizer dart. I'm gonna make that big guy
the spokesman for my new shoe store, Heel of
the Century Shoe Megaplex.

"People will travel from all corners of the globe and Idaho to see the giant feet of Bigfoot—and buy some cute leather tennis shoes with baby blue trim while they're at it."

To get Bigfoot's attention, the Spudscouts performed a loud ritual with bongos, gongs, and bagpipes.

"Wow!" said Grampa. "Not only are these Spudscouts crazed criminals, but they're talented musicians as well."

But Merle wasn't having any of it. He picked
the lock on our door with his pinky claw and
freed us.

"I didn't know Merle could pick locks," I said.

"Sure!" said Grampa. "He used to be a cat burglar."

Then Merle headed toward Gramma, silently
swimming through a murky pond.

He swung through the trees above the Spudscouts like a super feline ninja.

Then he used his master disguise talents to slip right by the Spudscouts unnoticed!

Merle leaped onto one of the poles and started to chew through Gramma's ropes. But it was too late! Bigfoot burst out of the trees and headed toward them.

"Gnaw faster, Merle!" yelled Gramma. "Gnaw like you've never gnawed before!"

"There he is!" yelled Spudmaster Maximus.
"Fire the Snooze Missile!"

The giant dart launched into the air like a
giant torpedo.

But Bigfoot just swiped it away like a pesky mosquito, and it veered off course.

Bigfoot reached toward Gramma . . . and grabbed Merle instead! The furry beast turned and ran off with Merle.

"I guess Bigfoot's more of a cat person," said Jubal.

# CHAPTER 10

# Kickin' into Gears

The Spudscouts, angry that we had messed up their plans, came after us.

"Let's turn these Spuds into mashed potatoes!" I yelled as I gave one of the attacking scouts a swift roundhouse kick. To my surprise, his head flew off and out popped nuts and bolts and some AAA batteries!

"Hey!" I yelled. "These Spudscouts aren't even real!"

"That's right," said Maximus as he pulled out a remote control. "I've constructed an entire robot Spud troop out of old computer parts and used blenders, which means they're highly intelligent and can make a mean mango smoothie. Now, prepare to meet the fury of the Robo Spuds!"

The Robo Spuds first attacked by forming a
Whirling Spudball of Doom.

But Jubal and I deflected it with our own world-
famous Human Twirly Bird Maneuver.

Next, the Robo Spuds attacked in a high-kickin' line-dance formation, singing selected songs from *Annie*, the musical.

But Gramma and I took care of them. "Now, normally I don't support using martial arts on eight-year-olds, but since these are robots, I guess it's okay!"

But there were too many of those darn Robo Spuds. We were surrounded.

"Resistance is futile!" said Maximus. "My highly trained Robo Spuds will attack you like a school of killer piranha!"

"Ha!" I yelled. "They obviously haven't seen the smoking karate skills of my Grampa! Hey! Where is Grampa, anyway?"

Grampa was napping.

"I was wondering what happened to my giant tranquilizer dart," said Maximus.

# CHAPTER 11

# Call of the Wild

"Let's face it," said Maximus. "You're trapped like poor, defenseless animals."

"Animals!" said Gramma. "That gives me an idea."

Now, anyone who lives in Gingham County knows that Gramma is a champion hog caller. She's won the annual hog-callin' competition for five years straight.

Gramma let out the mother of all hog calls. It sounded like a yodeling hippopotamus being hit by a steam engine!

HooHooEEEEE!!!

Suddenly, all the critters of the forest came to our rescue! Spudmaster Maximus and his Robo Spuds were attacked by squirrels, rats, birds, and Peruvian pygmy bats.

"It's lucky for you that I'm terrified of small birds and mammals!" yelled Maximus as he ran for the hills. "You haven't seen the last of me!"

Before we could go find Merle, I had to pull the giant dart from Grampa's foot.

"This doesn't seem safe," said Grampa as I tied one end of a rope to the dart and the other to a rock.

"Relax," I said. "It'll only sting for a second." And I threw the rock off a cliff.

# CHAPTER 12

# The Quest for Merle

After Grampa stopped shrieking, we prepared
to go rescue Merle. Gramma was highly upset.
She jumped up on a cliff and screamed, "I swear
by everything that I hold sacred, including
casseroles and soap operas, that I will find
you, Merle!"

Suddenly, I spotted Bigfoot.

"Look!" I yelled. "Bigfoot's taking Merle to the top of the Devil's Rump!"

"What a **bummer!**" yelled Grampa.

So we climbed after them.

"Be careful!" I said. "This Rump is big and unstable."

"You're telling me!" said Grampa.

We found Jubal toward the top of the mountain.

"How the heck did you beat us up here?" asked Grampa.

"Oh, I took the escalator," said Jubal. "It was much less tiring."

# CHAPTER 13

# Cat Rescue Squad

We quietly snuck up to peer over the edge of the mountain and spy on Bigfoot.

"Here," said Gramma. "Use these binoculars I made out of two old jelly jars."

It looked like Bigfoot and Merle were hitting it off.

"Bigfoot's got Merle!" said Grampa. "And he's playing the string game with him. And Merle looks like he's enjoying it!"

"Oh, I can't stand it!" said Gramma.

We had to go in and get Merle, and the only way to do it was to camouflage ourselves. I smeared mud and twigs on my face.

Jubal bravely added some cactus to his ensemble.

Gramma disguised herself as her favorite shrub, the highly toxic white oleander.

And Grampa disguised himself as a wise old tree wizard.

"What?" said Grampa. "I thought we were playing dress up."

We made our move. Jubal and I softly sang
Bigfoot to sleep with a beautiful rendition of
"Rock-a-Bye, Baby" while Grampa and Gramma
moved in.

Grampa used two stones to light some twigs
under Bigfoot's stinky foot.

"Whooo-eeee!" said Grampa. "These feet smell
worse than your Gramma's bleu cheese and
buttermilk soufflé!"

"I heard that!" said Gramma.

Bigfoot got a rude awakening, and he dropped Merle.

Luckily, Gramma was there to cushion Merle's fall with her big, bushy bun.

# A Case of the Runs

Once we got Merle, we did what any crack rescue team would do—we ran screaming for our lives! Bigfoot was hot on our tails.

But we quickly came to the edge of the Devil's Rump. Things weren't looking too good.

"I don't guess they've got a down escalator," I said.

# Air Spud

Suddenly, Spudmaster Maximus flew in with his Robo Spuds!

"Well, well, well!" said Maximus. "You aren't so tough without your army of squirrels and fluffy bunnies, are you! I knew you'd lead us straight to Bigfoot. Now we're gonna grab that big galoot!"

Several of the flying Robo Spuds swarmed Bigfoot like a cloud of gnats, to distract him.

"I'm gonna show you a little maneuver I learned from watching *Top Gun* twenty-five times!" said Maximus as he led his Spud squadron in a steep dive at full speed.

But even flying Robo Spuds were no match for Bigfoot's big feet. The beast gave them a mighty kick, sending them flying.

The Spuds were hurled into the chasm between the two cheeks of the Devil's Rump.

"Don't worry!" said Maximus. "There's nothing to be ashamed of, Spudscouts. We have created the world's biggest wedgie! We'll be famous!"

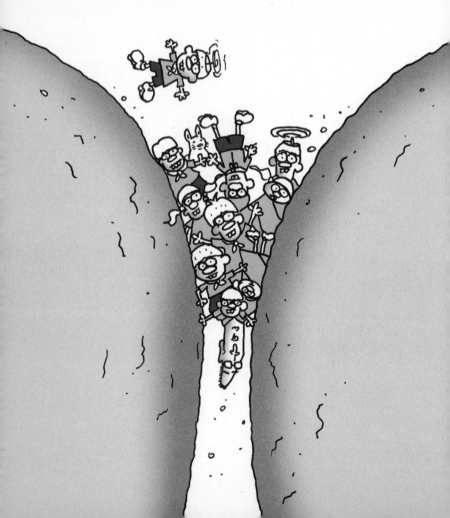

# CHAPTER 16

# The End is Near

So there we were, trapped again by Bigfoot.

"Let's just give Merle back to him," said Grampa. "We can get a new pet. Maybe an iguana or one of those hissing cockroaches."

But, to our surprise, a helicopter popped up from behind the cliff! It was Channel 5's smarmy weatherman, Blue Norther, in his Whopper Doppler Chopper.

"Hop in, folks!" said Blue Norther. "I'm here to bravely pluck you from the jagged jaws of danger!"

"I don't get it," said Grampa as we flew off to safety. "How did Blue Norther know we were in trouble?"

"Oh, I called him," said Gramma. "With this cell phone I made out of pebbles and tree moss."

# CHAPTER 17

# That's News to Me

Of course, our story of survival turned up on the news that night.

"And that, folks," said Blue Norther, "is how I single-handedly put the smackdown on Bigfoot and saved the family of inexperienced campers. It's a miracle I was able to fit this rescue into my busy schedule."

"Oh, brother!" I moaned.

"You know, I'm gonna miss that place," said
Grampa. "Beautiful scenery, interesting wildlife,
nonstop monster excitement, a giant rock
shaped like a butt—I think we should go back
there for spring break."

So that's all there is, folks.

For restoring the good name of the Spudscouts, Grampa was finally given the Silver Spud medal he had always wanted.

For tarnishing the good name of the Spudscouts, Spudmaster Maximus was given the Big Jerk medal he deserved and relocated to the Arctic Circle.

The Spudscouts were reprogrammed by top scientists and now perform in the popular Robo Spuds on Ice show every Wednesday and Saturday. Get your tickets now!

And after his upsetting kidnapping experience, Merle just needed some time to himself in a peaceful place where he could relax and recover...

**Wait a minute!** This story's not over yet. It turns out that Bigfoot tracked Merle all the way home and kidnapped him yet again!

"Help!" I yelled. "Bigfoot just interrupted Merle while he was trying to do his business!"

"I know just how he feels!" yelled Grampa from the bathroom.

# CHAPTER 18

# On the Town with Bigfoot

Bigfoot took poor Merle downtown and started to tear up the place. He even used a city bus as a skateboard.

"Can't he read the 'No Skateboarding' sign?" yelled the local military guy. "Let's blast him!"

"Nooooo!" shouted Gramma. "You'll blow up my cat!

# CHAPTER 19

# Helping Hans

"Vait a doggone minute!" said a voice in a funny accent. It was escaped criminal mastermind Hans Lotion and his grandson, Jurgen! Everyone jumped back in horror. "Don't be afraid! I can help you calm ze savage beast vithout exploding ze cute kitty cat!"

"Ze source of Bigfoot's anger is his feet," said Hans. "Based on ze crusty nature and ze smell of de feet, I have determined zat he suffers from *Tinea Pedis*, or 'athlete's foot' for all of you do-do brains out zere. Ve must relieve ze suffering in his feet."

"And why should we trust a crazed criminal like you?" asked Grampa.

"Because I used to be a foot doctor and I vill not allow my beloved city to be destroyed by a hairy monkey man. If anyvone is going to destroy zis town, it vill be me!"

Ze Human Foot

Picass

Bigfoot's athlete's foot gave me an idea. I ran over to the local construction sight.

"Everyone, get over here!" I yelled. "Grab some lumber and some paint and some hammers!"

"Are we remodeling the bathroom?" asked Grampa.

"No! I've got a plan to save Merle and capture Bigfoot without any more carnage."

"Sounds kinda boring," complained Grampa.

# CHAPTER 20

# A Little of the Bubbly

We all headed to Manny's Hot Tub Plantation for a little renovation. Manny wasn't too crazy about it.

"Hey guys!" yelled Officer Brightwell.
"Bigfoot's eating the Krispy Scream donut
shop! That's a national landmark. We've really
gotta blow him up!"

But we had other plans.

"Yo! Bigfoot!" I yelled.

"Come and soak your dogs in this hot, soothing footbath! That's right! It's the world's largest, made for the biggest, stinkiest, itchiest feet in the world!"

Bigfoot couldn't resist. He ran over to us.

Bigfoot jumped in the footbath and let out a sigh of relief. The big guy seemed happy as he soothed his fungus-filled feet.

But he was in for a surprise!

"That's not soothing medicated water!" I yelled. "That's quick-drying cement. Now we've got you, you big bully cat thief!"

Bigfoot was stuck. With some strategic tickling we got him to drop Merle and have a good laugh.

# CHAPTER 21

# Hugs, Fungus, and Bugs

Merle was reunited with his beloved family, again, and Gramma gave him a big bear hug.

"Careful, Granny!" said Grampa. "Don't squeeze him too hard. The way I figure, that cat's only got one of his nine lives left!"

Okay, so that's the end of my story. For real.
Bigfoot was dropped back on top of the
Devil's Rump with a year's supply of itchy foot
ointment.

Grampa gave him a new kitty.

"Here ya go," said Grampa.
"His name's Jo-Jo. Try not to eat him!"

And Hans was rewarded by the mayor for helping to save the town from destruction. All of his previous charges were dropped, and he was allowed to reopen his doctor's office.

"I still don't trust that mustached menace," said Grampa.

"I don't know," I said. "I think he's changed his evil ways. Maybe deep down underneath, Hans is a really good guy."

Boy, was I wrong.

World-famous nature photographer Possum Lixum snapped these two shots of Bigfoot, but something's not quite right with that second picture. Help our scientists pick out the differences before they're published in *Natural Geographic* magazine.

The answers are on the next page. Anyone caught cheating will be forced to give Bigfoot a stinky foot massage!